This book is dedicated to my three amazing children,
Malakai, Lucas, and Olivia, and my spectacular wife,
Karen, with whom I get to share this amazing parenting
journey. I love our little pod!

Published in the United States by: Hay House, Inc.: www.hayhouse.com®
Published in Australia by: Hay House Australia Pty. Ltd.: www.hayhouse.com.au
Published in the United Kingdom by: Hay House UK, Ltd.: www.hayhouse.co.uk
Published in India by: Hay House Publishers India: www.hayhouse.co.in

Cover & Interior design: designbylovelyday.com • Interior photos/illustrations: Erin Mariano

Library of Congress Control Number: 2016953865

Hardcover ISBN: 978-1-4019-5287-7

12 11 10 9 8 7 6 5 4 3
1st edition, December 2016

Printed in the United States of America

SUSTAINABLE FORESTRY INITIATIVE
Certified Sourcing
www.sfiprogram.org
SFI-01268
SFI label applies to text stock only

Gorilla Thumps & Bear Hugs

A Tapping Solution Children's Story

by Alex Ortner ★ Illustrations by Erin Mariano

One day during recess, Lucas noticed that his friend Annabel looked very sad.

When he asked her what was wrong, she said, "I was drawing a picture of myself as a scientist, and two kids teased me. They told me the picture was silly and that I was crazy for wanting to be a scientist. But I think science is so much fun! 3

"I want to be an astronomer so I can learn about fun stuff like the billions of stars in space.

4

"Or maybe a zoologist, studying all the different animals in the world, where they live and what they do.

"Or a doctor, learning about all the amazing things in our bodies, like our eyes that see, our ears that hear, our lungs that breathe, and our hearts that beat.

"But kids are always teasing me for liking science. Maybe I am foolish for wanting to be a scientist. Maybe I'm not smart enough. Maybe that's why I'm so sad," Annabel said with a sigh.

"I'm sorry you're sad. I know a secret trick that might help you feel better," Lucas said.

"A few weeks ago I was really sad because I tripped and fell playing soccer. It hurt, and I didn't want to play anymore because I looked silly in front of my friends. So I quit.

"When my brother, Malakai, saw how sad I was, he taught me something called the Magical Tapping Technique, and it made me feel much better. Want to learn about it?"

"Sure," Annabel said.

"He started by telling me that we all have magical points on our bodies where we can touch our energy," Lucas said, "and that by tapping on these points while saying magic words, we can change how we feel. He has really fun ways to remember each point."

8

HIYAH!

"We always start the tapping with the
KARATE CHOP POINT," Malakai said as
he tapped on the outside of his hand. "With this point,
I like to think about doing karate and breaking a board.

"Next is the Eyebrow Point," he said. "I call this the
HAIRY EYEBROW POINT.

When I tap here, I pretend that I have eyebrows so big that birds can land on them and sing songs to make me feel better.

"Then there's the Side of the Eye Point, which I call the
SUPER EAGLE EYE POINT.

When I tap here, I pretend I have super eagle eyes
that let me look at things in a different way.

11

"Next is the Under Eye Point. I call this the
LION CRY POINT.

This helps me remember that even if you're as strong
as a lion, it's still okay to cry and let bad feelings out.
A lot of times, crying makes you feel better.

"Then there's the Under the Nose Point—
THE DRAGON FIRE POINT.

When I tap here, I pretend I'm a dragon setting fire to my bad feelings as I breathe them out of my nose. I can feel the bad feelings leaving through the hot fire on my hands as I tap.

Ahhhh
Awwooooooo!

"Next is the Chin Point. I call this the
WOLF'S CHIN POINT

because when I tap here I think about
a wolf howling away the bad feelings.

"Then there's the Collarbone Point, which I think of as the GORILLA THUMP POINT.

When I tap here, it's like I'm a big, proud gorilla beating on my chest.

"Next is the Underarm Point. I call this the **BEAR HUG POINT** because when I tap here I think about giving myself lots of love with a big bear hug!

"And the last one is the Top of Head Point. I call this the MONKEY POINT.

When I tap on this point, I like to pretend I'm a monkey. Sometimes I even make monkey sounds!"

"Malakai showed me how to tap on each magical point on my body with my fingers while saying the magical words," Lucas said. "At first I felt silly, and I even giggled, thinking about the funny names for each point, but once I started doing it, I didn't mind because it made me feel so much better."

"That sounds like it could help, but what are the magical words?" Annabel asked.

"They're actually called Magical Tapping Phrases," said Lucas. "You say them when you're tapping on the Magical Energy Points. Basically you just say out loud how you're feeling, and this helps the feelings change."

"Can we try it?" said Annabel.

"Sure. Just repeat after me and tap where I tap," answered Lucas.

"First, tap on the Karate Chop Point and say, 'Even though I feel sad because some kids teased me about my pictures, I love myself anyway.'" Annabel did just what he said.

"Keep tapping and say this two times: 'Even though I feel sad because some kids teased me, I'm a good kid anyway.'" Annabel repeated what Lucas said twice.

"Great," said Lucas. "Now let's go to the Hairy Eyebrow Point and say,
'I feel sad because the kids teased me.'"

Lucas and Annabel continued to tap on each point, saying the Magical Tapping
Phrases. Soon Annabel got the hang of it and started tapping on her own.

When Annabel finished tapping through
all the points, Lucas told her to take a deep
breath in. . . and then out.

"How do you feel?" he asked.

"Wow! I feel a lot better," she said. "This is magic. . . real magic.
And you know what? I had a great idea when we were tapping."
Annabel got up and said, "I have to go ask the teacher about my idea!"

After recess, the teacher asked all the kids to draw pictures of what they wanted to be when they grew up. They all had different ideas, like being a police officer or a teacher or a firefighter or an artist or an astronaut or a professional soccer player. Of course, Annabel drew herself as a scientist.

When they were done, each kid got to share his or her picture with the class and tell why they chose that job. Everyone had an amazing time! And Annabel was no longer alone.

The next day Annabel came up to Lucas and said, "Thank you for showing me the Magical Tapping Technique. It made me feel so much better and even helped me have the idea for us all to draw our dreams!"

"You're welcome," Lucas said. "I'm glad you liked it. Malakai and I are starting a Tapping Club to teach other kids how to tap. Do you want to help?"

"I'd love to," Annabel said with a big grin.

LET'S TAP!
Using the Magical Tapping Technique with Your Child

Tell Me More about Tapping. . .
Tapping is a seamless blend of ancient Chinese acupressure and Western psychology. In children and adults, it relieves stress and anxiety, increases focus and calm, promotes restful sleep, healthy emotional expression, physical and emotional healing and wellness, as well as pain relief, trauma relief, and more.

How Does Tapping Relieve Stress?
Tapping quickly disrupts the body's stress response. In a double-blind research study, Tapping decreased levels of the stress hormone cortisol in the body by an average of 24%. Some study participantsexperienced a 50% decrease in one hour of tapping.

By lowering cortisol, which is responsible for putting the body and mind into a stressed state, Tapping supports physical and emotional well-being. In this relaxed state, we're better able to **heal, experience restorative sleep, healthy metabolism, pain relief,** as well as a **positive state of mind,** and **more.**

If you're ready to try Tapping with your child, here are some quick tips:

* **Always get your child's okay first.** If they're unwilling to tap, wait for another time. (And if their resistance makes you anxious, tap on it!)

* **If your child can't or won't tap on the points themselves,** as long as they're willing to tap, feel free to tap through their points for them. If they think you're tickling them, feel free to share a giggle! Then focus on the points that are less ticklish.

* **If your child thinks tapping is a game, go with it!** Tapping doesn't need to feel serious to produce great results. Say silly things, include their stuffed animals and imaginary characters, and more.

* **If your child can't sit still,** move along with them and have them mimic you as you tap through the points alongside them. One of the great things about Tapping is that it requires movement, which kids often do naturally.

* **If you're unsure how to get started, start with what your child is experiencing at that moment.** Whether it's challenging emotions, high energy at bedtime, or another issue, take a moment and do some tapping on it.

Tapping with Your Child at Bedtime

Tapping is a great practice to incorporate at bedtime, since it promotes **mental, emotional,** and **physical relaxation.** To have a positive first experience with this new Magical Tapping Technique, first ask their permission. If they're willing, begin tapping on the **Karate Chop (KC) point:**

Karate Chop: Even though I'm not sure I'm ready to sleep yet, I love myself and I'm okay.
Karate Chop: Even though it's time to sleep and I'm not sure I'm ready, I'm a great kid and I'm okay.
Karate Chop: Even though I'm not sure I'm ready to sleep, I love myself and I'm okay.

Hairy Eyebrow Point (Eyebrow): Not sure I'm ready to sleep
Super Eagle Eye (Side of Eye): But it's my bedtime
Lion Cry (Under Eye): Not sure I'm ready to sleep
Dragon Fire (Under Nose): That's okay
Wolf's Chin (Under Mouth): I'm a great kid!
Gorilla Thump (Collarbone): I can feel quiet now
Bear Hug (Under Arm): I can feel calm now
Monkey Point (Top of Head): Feeling calm and quiet now
Hairy Eyebrow Point (Eyebrow): Time to sleep
Super Eagle Eye (Side of Eye): Sleep feels good!
Lion Cry (Under Eye): Time to sleep
Dragon Fire (Under Nose): Feeling calm and quiet now
Wolf's Chin (Under Mouth): Letting myself feel quiet inside now
Gorilla Thump (Collarbone): Relaxing my body now
Bear Hug (Under Arm): Feeling quiet all over
Monkey Point (Top of Head): Letting myself settle down now

Hairy Eyebrow Point (Eyebrow): Feeling calm
Super Eagle Eye (Side of Eye): Ready to sleep
Lion Cry (Under Eye): Feeling calm and quiet now
Dragon Fire (Under Nose): I can go to sleep easily now
Wolf's Chin (Under Mouth): Letting myself go to sleep
Gorilla Thump (Collarbone): Feeling calm and quiet
Bear Hug (Under Arm): Feeling ready to sleep now
Monkey Point (Top of Head): Feeling quiet and sleepy all over

> ⭐ **Keep tapping** until your child is ready to sleep or already asleep.

There are many different reasons adults struggle with consistently getting restorative sleep. For some people, it's their child awakening at night that interferes with sleep. Others may struggle with quieting their mind at night, or with overcoming physical discomfort or pain.

In this tapping script, we'll focus on releasing stress so that you can relax more quickly at night. By regularly using tapping to quiet your mind and body before sleep, you're more likely to wake up feeling rested and energized.

First take a deep breath, and then begin tapping on the Karate Chop point:
Take a deep breath. Keep tapping until you feel calm and ready to sleep.

KC: Even though I'm not yet relaxed enough to fall asleep, I love myself and accept how I feel.
KC: Even though my mind is still buzzing and my body won't relax, I deeply and completely love and accept myself.
KC: Even though it's time to sleep but I'm not yet fully relaxed, I love myself and accept how I feel.

Eyebrow: It's time to sleep
Side of Eye: But my mind won't stop buzzing
Under Eye: And my body feels tense
Under Nose: I need to relax
Under Mouth: But it's not always that easy
Collarbone: My mind won't stop going
Under Arm: And my body won't relax
Top of Head: It's time to get some sleep

Eyebrow: But it's hard to quiet the mental noise
Side of Eye: And relax my body
Under Eye: I hope my child sleeps through the night
Under Nose: It's so frustrating being woken up
Under Mouth: All this stress and frustration
Collarbone: I can let myself feel it all
Under Arm: And let it all go now
Top of Head: I can feel relaxed and comfortable in my body now

Eyebrow: I can let go of all these busy thoughts
Side of Eye: And release any stress I may be feeling
Under Eye: Letting go of whatever happened today
Under Nose: And releasing stress about tomorrow too
Under Mouth: Quieting my mind and body now
Collarbone: Allowing myself to feel quiet and comfortable
Under Arm: Fully relaxing my mind and body now
Top of Head: Feeling complete peace and quiet in mind and body

Take a deep breath. Keep tapping until you feel calm and ready to sleep.

★ **Note:** *It's important to tap through what you're feeling emotionally and in your body and mind, so feel free to change the words to match your experience.*

If you want to see a video on how to do Tapping, check out this quick 4-minute video on our website:

thetappingsolution.com/kids/how-to-tap

Enjoy!

Some Free Resources for You!

As a special thank you for purchasing this children's book, I want to give you a few free resources that I know both you and your children can benefit from right away.

These include free tapping meditations (like a great tapping for stress relief meditation), articles, videos, and much more. You can access them all on this page:

thetappingsolution.com/kids/resources

Also make sure to check out some of our other *New York Times* bestselling books (for both children and adults!) by going here:

thetappingsolution.com/books

We have books on topics such as weight loss and body confidence, pain relief, tapping for teenagers, and much more!

We hope you enjoyed this Hay House book. If you'd like to receive our online catalog featuring additional information on Hay House books and products, or if you'd like to find out more about the Hay Foundation, please contact:

Hay House, Inc., P.O. Box 5100, Carlsbad, CA 92018-5100
(760) 431-7695 or (800) 654-5126
(760) 431-6948 (fax) or (800) 650-5115 (fax)
www.hayhouse.com® • www.hayfoundation.org

Published in Australia by: Hay House Australia Pty. Ltd.,
18/36 Ralph St., Alexandria NSW 2015 • *Phone:* 612-9669-4299
Fax: 612-9669-4144 • www.hayhouse.com.au

Published in the United Kingdom by: Hay House UK, Ltd.,
The Sixth Floor, Watson House, 54 Baker Street, London W1U 7BU
Phone: +44 (0)20 3927 7290 • Fax: +44 (0)20 3927 7291 • www.hayhouse.co.uk

Published in India by: Hay House Publishers India, Muskaan Complex, Plot No. 3, B-2,
Vasant Kunj, New Delhi 110 070 • *Phone:* 91-11-4176-1620
Fax: 91-11-4176-1630 • www.hayhouse.co.in

<u>Access New Knowledge.</u>
<u>Anytime. Anywhere.</u>

Learn and evolve at your own pace
with the world's leading experts.

www.hayhouseU.com